BOTTOMLEY
the Brave

Peter Harris
& Doffy Weir

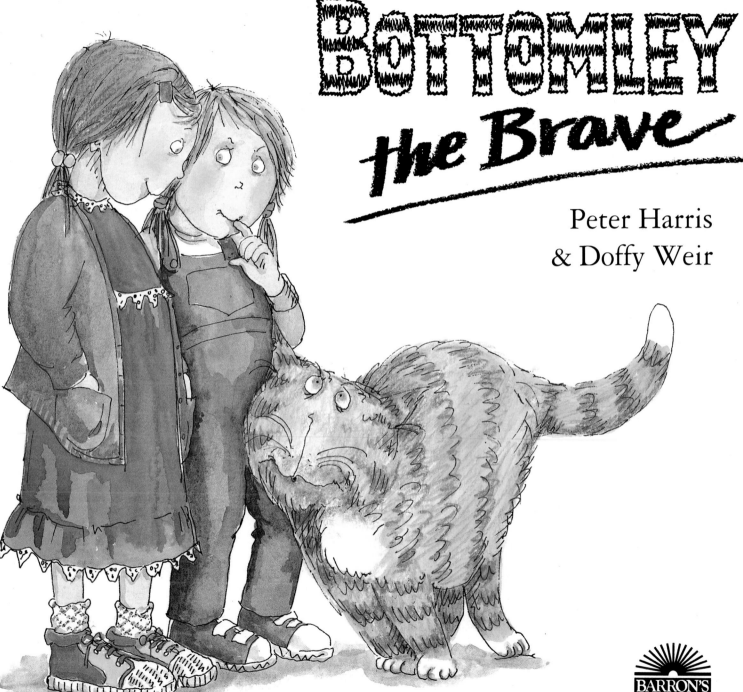

BARRON'S

It doesn't take much to wake me.

Bottomley
the Brave

So I was on my feet the moment
the six burglars broke in.

Of course, they knew they'd made a big
mistake as soon as they saw me.

"Quick! Run for it!" one burglar screamed. "That's no ordinary cat! That's Bottomley!"

"Bottomley the Brave."

But I wasn't going to let them get away that easily.

I attacked them in a second, clawing and biting.

Well, the fight didn't last long.

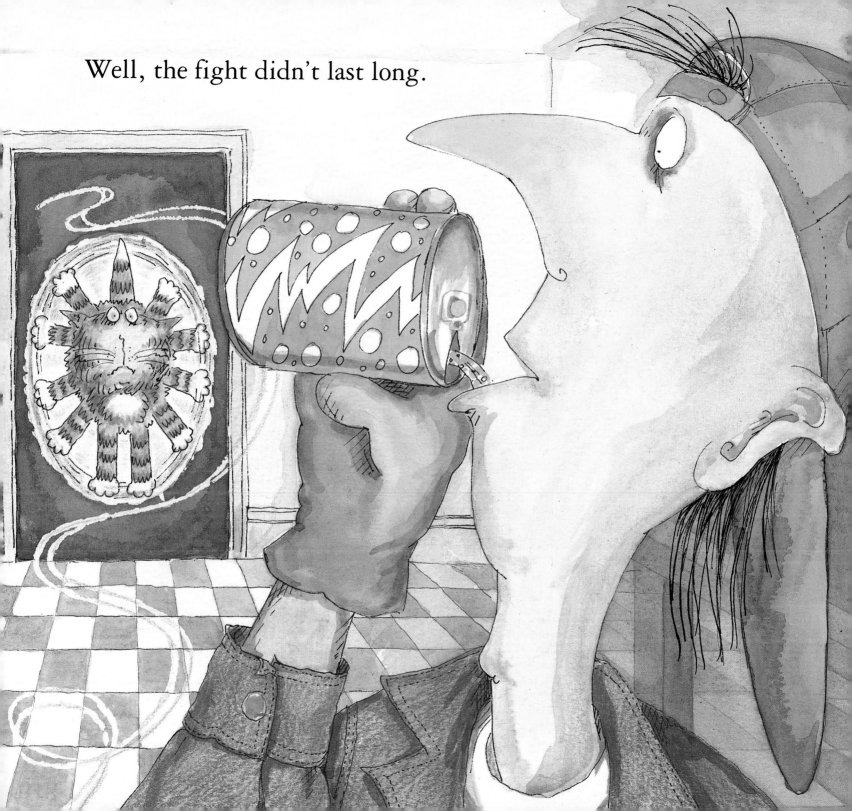

Because I don't think they'd met
a cat who knew karate before.

And pretty soon four of them
were begging for mercy.

The other two tried to run for it.

But they didn't stand a chance.

Who would against a trained
fighting cat like me?

And then I just called for the police
to come and arrest them.

But the bad news is, while
I was clobbering the last
two burglars, the other four
ate that roast chicken you
were saving for supper
and escaped.

"You believe me, don't you?"
"No, Bottomley. Not one word.

But we do believe you are the laziest, sleepiest, greediest, funniest cat . . .

. . . who tells the best stories in the world."

For Chris — P.H.

To Skeff, in memory of Douglas who loved cats — D.W.

First edition for the United States
published by Barron's Educational Series, Inc., 1996.

First published in Great Britain in 1996 by
Hutchinson Children's Books
Random House UK Limited
20 Vauxhall Bridge Road
London SW1V 2SA

All inquiries should be addressed to:
Barron's Educational Series, Inc.,
250 Wireless Boulevard
Hauppauge, New York 11788

Library of Congress Catalog Card No. 96-83059

ISBN 0-8120-9785-8

Printed in China

6789 2997 987654321